Words to Know Before You Read

concentration

dejected

endangered

gallant

gazed

glumly

habitat

kingdom

riffle

www.rourkepublishing.com

Edited by Luana K. Mitten
Illustrated by Ed Myer
Art Direction and Page Layout by Renee Brady

Library of Congress Cataloging-in-Publication Data

Steinkraus, Kyla
 The Tree Fort / Kyla Steinkraus.
   p. cm. -- (Little Birdie Books)
 ISBN 978-1-61741-834-1 (hard cover) (alk. paper)
 ISBN 978-1-61236-038-6 (soft cover)
 Library of Congress Control Number: 2011924723

Rourke Publishing
Printed in the United States of America, North Mankato, Minnesota
060711
060711CL

www.rourkepublishing.com - rourke@rourkepublishing.com
Post Office Box 643328 Vero Beach, Florida 32964

The Tree Fort

By Kyla Steinkraus

Illustrated by Ed Myer

Will and his sister Jessie liked to play outside. They enjoyed the tire swing, the swimming pool, and the basketball net.

But most of all they loved the tree fort
in the forest beyond their backyard.

5

Usually they played with their best friends, Sophie and Max. But today everyone was sad. The forest was going to be cut down to build a mall.

"I can't believe they're tearing down our fort," Will said glumly.

"I wish we could save it," whispered Sophie.

7

Jessie tied a balloon to the railing and watched it bob in the breeze. "We could tie a million balloons to the fort until it floats away!"

"We could float it down into our backyard, right Max?" asked Sophie.

8

Max just shook his head and looked down at his bird watching book. He was too dejected to imagine anything.

Will picked up a cardboard sword and swung it. "I wish I could be a real knight."

10

Jessie leaned out the window and gazed up at the sky. A bird chirped in the tree next to her. "Maybe a giant eagle could land and fly the fort away on his back."

"Or a dragon!" Will added.

Max looked at the bird outside the window. It was much smaller than an eagle or a dragon.
He'd seen a bird like that somewhere.

13

"What if there could be a huge wave of—of—of ice cream!" Sophie exclaimed.

"The fort could ride the wave all the way to our house!" she added.

"What do you think, Max?" Will asked. Max riffled through his bird book with great concentration.

14

15

Max looked up with a grin. "I don't think we need knights or balloons or giant eagles. I think this little brown bird will do."

16

"What do you mean?" asked Sophie.

Max pointed to his book. "See? This bird right outside our fort is endangered."

17

"How is it in danger?" Jessie asked.

Max smiled. "Endangered means there aren't many left. Our forest is a protected habitat!"

18

Jessie leaped up. "If they can't cut down our forest, they can't destroy our tree fort!"

19

The four friends scrambled down the ladder. They couldn't wait to tell their parents. There would be many more afternoons of mighty dragons and gallant knights after all.

After Reading Activities

You and the Story...

What was going to happen to the tree fort?

How did the kids save the tree fort?

Have you ever tried to save something that was going to be destroyed?

Tell a friend what you would do if something you liked was going to be destroyed.

Words You Know Now...

Write a new story. Choose three words from the list below to include in your opening paragraph.

concentration	glumly
dejected	habitat
endangered	kingdom
gallant	riffled
gazed	

You Could... Make a Plan to Help an Endangered Animal

- Research what animals are considered endangered.

- Choose one animal from the endangered animals list.

- Decide what you will do to help inform people about this animal.
  Here are some ideas:
    - Make a brochure with facts about this animal.
    - Write a letter to an animal rights group.
    - Write letters to friends and relatives informing them about the
      endangered animal.

About the Author

Kyla Steinkraus lives in Tampa with her husband and two children. She never had a tree fort growing up, but she and her friends would make tree hammocks by tying blankets between two branches.

About the Illustrator

Ed Myer is a Manchester-born illustrator now living in London. After growing up in an artistic household, Ed studied ceramics at university but always continued drawing pictures. As well as illustration, Ed likes travelling, playing computer games and walking little ted (his Jack russell).